Kidnapped

BY R. L. STEVENSON

Illustrated by Bill McKibbon
Retold by Derek Lord

McClelland and Stewart Limited
Toronto   Montreal

I will begin the story of my adventure with a certain morning early in the month of June, the year of grace 1751, when I took the key for the last time out of the door of my father's house. Mr. Campbell, the minister of Essendean, was waiting for me.

"Well, Davie, lad," said he, "I will go with you as far as the ford, to set you on the way and tell your fortune. When your mother was gone, and your father (the worthy Christian man) began to sicken for his end, he gave me in charge a certain letter, which he said was your inheritance. 'So soon,' says he, 'as I am gone, give my boy this letter into his hand, and start him off to the house of Shaws, not far from Cramond'."

"The house of Shaws!" I cried. "What had my poor father to do with the house of Shaws?"

"Nay," said Mr. Campbell, "who can tell that for a surety? But the name of that family, Davie, boy, is the name you bear — Balfour of Shaws."

He gave me the letter, which was addressed in these words: "To the hands of Ebenezer Balfour, Esq., of Shaws, in his house of Shaws, these will be delivered by my son, David Balfour."

With that, Mr. Campbell, good friend that he was, prayed a little while aloud for a young man setting out into the world; then held me at arm's length, looking at me with his face all working with sorrow; and then whipped about, and crying goodbye to me, set off by the way that we had come.

On the forenoon of the second day, coming to the top of a hill, I saw all the country fall away before me down to the sea; and in the midst of this descent, on a long ridge, the city of Edinburgh smoking like a kiln.

Presently after, I came by a house where a shepherd lived, and got a rough direction for the neighbourhood of Cramond; and so, from one to another worked my way to the westward of the capital by Colinton, till I came out upon the Glasgow road.

It was drawing on to sundown when I met a stout, dark,

sour-looking woman coming trudging down a hill; and she, when I asked the whereabouts of Shaws, turned sharp about, accompanied me back to the summit she had just left, and pointed to a great bulk of building standing very bare upon a green in the bottom of the next valley. The country was pleasant round about, but the house itself appeared to be a kind of ruin. My heart sank. "That!" I cried.

The woman's face lit up with a malignant anger. "That is the house of Shaws!" she cried. "I spit upon the ground, and

crack my thumb at it! Black be its fall! If ye see the laird, tell him that Jennet Clouston has called down the curse on him, and his house, byre and stable, man, guest, and master, wife, miss, or bairn—black, black be their fall!"

And the woman turned with a skip, and was gone. I stood for some minutes where she left me, with my hair on end.

Then I set forward by a little faint track in the grass that led in my direction; but the nearer I got to Shaws, the drearier it appeared. It seemed like the one wing of a house that had never been finished. What should have been the inner end

stood open on the upper floors, and showed against the sky
with steps and stairs of uncompleted masonry.

The door, as well as I could see it in the dim light, was a
great piece of wood all studded with nails; and I lifted my
hand, with a faint heart under my jacket, and knocked once.
Then I stood and waited. I knocked again, but whoever was
in that house kept deadly still, for I could hear nothing but the
ticking of a clock.

I began to rain kicks and buffets on the door, and to shout
out aloud for Mr. Balfour. I was in full career, when I heard
a cough right overhead, and, jumping back and looking up,
beheld a man's head in a tall night-cap, and the bell mouth
of a blunderbuss, at one of the first-storey windows.

"It's loaded," said a voice.

"I have come here with a letter," I said, "to Mr. Ebenezer Balfour of Shaws."

"Who are ye?" came the response.

"I am not ashamed of my name," said I. "They call me David Balfour."

It was after quite a long pause, and with a curious change of voice, that the next question followed:

"Is your father dead?"

I was so much surprised at this, that I could find no voice to answer, but stood staring.

"Ay," the man resumed, "He'll be dead, no doubt; and that'll be what brings ye chapping to my door. Well, man, I'll let ye in," and he disappeared from the window.

Presently there came a great rattling of chains and bolts, and the door was cautiously opened and shut to again behind me.

"Go into the kitchen and touch naething," said the voice; and while the person of the house set himself to replacing the defences of the door, I groped my way forward and entered the kitchen, the barest room I think I ever put my eyes on.

As soon as the last chain was up, the man rejoined me. He was a mean, stooping, narrow-shouldered, clay-faced creature; and his age might have been anything between fifty and seventy.

"Let's see the letter," said he.

I told him the letter was for Mr. Balfour: not for him.

"And who do ye think I am?" says he. "Give me Alexander's letter!"

"You know my father's name?"

"It would be strange if I didnae," he returned, "for he was my born brother. I'm your born uncle, Davie, my man, and you my born nephew."

Struck dumb with shock and disappointment, I handed him the letter.

"Do ye ken what's in it?" he asked suddenly.

"You see for yourself, sir," said I, "that the seal has not been broken."

"Ay," said he, "but what brought you here?"

"To give the letter," said I.

"No," says he cunningly, "but ye'll have had some hopes, nae doubt?"

"I confess, sir," said I, "when I was told that I had kinsfolk well-to-do, I did indeed indulge the hope that they might help me in my life. But I am no beggar; I look for no favours at your hands, and I want none that are not freely given."

"Hoot-toot!" said Uncle Ebenezer, "dinnae fly up in the snuff at me. We'll agree fine yet. But now come awa' to your bed, Davie."

To my surprise, he lit no lamp or candle, but set forth into the dark passage, groped his way, breathing deeply, up a flight of steps, and paused before a door, which he unlocked. I was

close upon his heels, having stumbled after as best I might; and then he bade me go in, for that was my chamber. I did as he bid, but paused after a few steps, and begged a light to go to bed with.

"Hoot-toot!" said Uncle Ebenezer, "there's a fine moon."

"Neither moon nor star, sir," said I. "I cannae see the bed."

"Hoot-toot!" said he. "Lights in a house is a thing I dinnae agree with. I'm unco feared of fires. Good night to ye, Davie, my man." And before I had time to add a further protest, he pulled the door to, and I heard him lock me in from the outside.

Next morning, I had to knock and shout to be let out of my miserable room, and then be content with a wash at a draw-well and a frugal breakfast of porridge. Then my uncle sat down in the sun at one of the windows and silently smoked a pipe.

"Davie, my man," said he, at last, "ye've come to the right bit when ye came to your Uncle Ebenezer. I mean to do the right by you; but while I'm taking a bit think to mysel' of what's the

best thing to put you to, I'll ask you to keep your tongue within your teeth. Nae letters; nae messages; no kind of word to ony-body; or else—there's my door."

"Uncle Ebenezer," I said, "you hate to have me in this house; you let me see it, every word and every minute; it's not possible that you can like me. Why do you seek to help me, then, and at the same time treat me like some sort of prisoner?"

"Na, na; na, na," he said, very earnestly. "I like you fine; we'll agree fine yet."

We were interrupted at this point by a knocking at the door.

Bidding my uncle sit where he was, I went to open it, and found on the doorstep a half-grown boy in sea-clothes.

"I've brought a letter from old Heasy-oasy to Mr. Belflower," he declared.

I brought him in and my uncle read the letter. Suddenly, the old man got to his feet with a great air of liveliness, and pulled me apart into the farthest corner of the room.

"Read that," said he, and put the following letter in my hand.

"The Hawes Inn, at the Queen's Ferry

"Sir,—I lie here with my hawser up and down, and send my cabin-boy to informe. If you have any further commands for over-seas, to-day will be the last occasion, as the wind will serve us well out of the firth. I will not seek to deny that I have had crosses with your agent, Mr. Rankeillor; of which, if not speedily redd up, you may looke to see some losses follow. I have drawn a bill upon you, as per margin, and am, sir, your most obedt., humble servant,

"Elias Hoseason."

"You see, Davie," resumed my uncle, "I have a venture with this man Hoseason, the captain of a trading brig, the *Covenant*, of Dysart. Now, if you and me was to walk over with yon lad, I could see the captain at the Hawes, or may be on board the *Covenant* if there was papers to be signed; and so far from a loss of time, we can jog on to the lawyer, Mr. Rankeillor's." My uncle went on to explain that Mr. Rankeillor was a highly respected man, whose word I could trust and who would put matters to rights between us.

"Very well," says I, "let us go to the Queen's Ferry."

When we came to the Hawes Inn, after a considerable walk, Ransome (Hoseason's ill-used and halfwitted cabin-boy) led us up the stair to a small room, heated like an oven by a great fire of coal. At a table hard by the chimney, a tall, dark, sober-looking man sat writing. In spite of the heat of the room, he wore a thick sea-jacket, buttoned to the neck, and a tall hairy cap drawn down over his ears.

He got to his feet at once, and offered his large hand to

Ebenezer. "I am proud to see you, Mr. Balfour," said he.

"Captain Hoseason," returned my uncle, "you keep your room unco hot."

"It's a habit I have, Mr. Balfour," said the skipper. "I have a cold blood, sir."

Though I had promised myself not to let my kinsman out of sight, I was so sickened by the closeness of the room, that when he told me to "run downstairs and play myself awhile," I was fool enough to take him at his word.

Away I went, therefore, and it occurred to me that, as the landlord was a man of that county, I might do well to make a friend of him. I asked him if he knew Mr. Rankeillor.

"Hoot, ay," says he, "and a very honest man."

I said it seemed that Ebenezer Balfour was ill-seen in the country.

"Nae doubt," said the landlord. "He's a wicked auld man and there's many would like to see him hanged. And yet he was once a fine young fellow, too. But that was before the report gaed abroad about Mr. Alexander; that was like the death of him."

"And what was it?" I asked.

"Ou, just that he had killed him," said the landlord. "Did ye never hear that?"

"And what would he kill him for?" said I.

"And what for, but just to get Shaws," said he.

"Aye, man?" said I. "Is that so? Was my—was Alexander the eldest son?"

"'Deed was he," said the landlord. "What else would he have killed him for?"

And with that he went away. I sat stunned with my good fortune: Shaws, and all the wealth of the estate, was mine by right of inheritance through my father, the elder son. It was now easy to see why Uncle Ebenezer disliked me, and would do all in his power to free himself of me, and of my claim to the property he had come to consider his own.

The next thing, I heard my uncle calling me, and found him outside with Hoseason.

"Mr. Balfour tells me great things of you," said the captain. "Ye shall come on board my brig for half an hour and drink a bowl with me."

Now, I longed to see the inside of a ship, but I was not going to put myself in jeopardy, and I told him my uncle and I had an appointment with a lawyer.

"Ay, ay," said he, "he passed me word of that. But, ye see, the boat'll set ye ashore at the town pier, and that's but a penny stonecast from Rankeillor's house."

By this time we were at the boat-side, and he was handing me in. As soon as we were alongside, Hoseason, declaring that he and I must be the first aboard, ordered a tackle to be sent down from the main-yard. In this I was whipped into the air and set down again on the deck, where the captain stood ready waiting for me.

"Where is my uncle?" said I, when he failed to follow us aboard.

"Ay," said Hoseason, with a sudden grimness, "That's the point."

I felt I was lost. With all my strength, I plucked myself clear of him and ran to the bulwarks. Sure enough, there was the boat pulling for the town, with my uncle sitting in the stern. I gave a piercing cry—"Help, help! Murder!"—so that both sides of the anchorage rang with it, and my uncle turned round where he was sitting, and showed me a face full of cruelty and terror.

It was the last I saw. Already strong hands had been plucking me back from the ship's side; and now a thunderbolt seemed to strike me; I saw a great flash of fire, and fell senseless.

I came to myself in darkness, in great pain, bound hand and foot, and deafened by many unfamiliar noises. There sounded in my ears a roaring of water, as of a huge mill-dam, the thrashing of heavy sprays, the thundering of the sails, and the shrill cries of seamen. I had no measure of time; day and night were alike in that ill-smelling cavern of the *Covenant's* bowels where I lay, but sleep at length stole from me the consciousness of sorrow.

I was wakened by the light of a hand-lantern shining in my face. A small man of about thirty, with green eyes and a tangle of fair hair, was bending over me, and beside him stood Captain Hoseason.

"Now, sir, you see for yourself," said the first: "A high fever, no light, no meat; you see for yourself what that means. I want that boy taken out of this hole and put in the forecastle."

"Are ye saying that the lad will die if he bides here, Mr.

Riach?" asked the captain.

"Aye, will he!"

"Well, sir," said Hoseason, "flit him where ye please!"

Five minutes afterwards my bonds were cut, I was hoisted on a man's back, carried up to the forecastle, and laid in a bunk on some sea-blankets; where the first thing that I did was to lose my senses.

It was a blessed thing indeed to open my eyes again upon the daylight, and to find myself in the society of men. The forecastle was a roomy place enough, set all about with berths, in which the men of the watch below were seated smoking, or lying down asleep.

Here I lay for the space of many days a close prisoner, and not only got my health again, but came to know my companions. They were a rough lot indeed, as sailors mostly are, and I learnt from them that the ship was bound for the Carolinas, where my uncle had condemned me to be sold into slavery on the plantations.

The cabin-boy, Ransome, came in at times from the round-house (the officers' quarters), where he berthed and served, now nursing a bruised limb in silent agony, now raving against the cruelty of Mr. Shuan, the chief mate. I found there was a strange peculiarity about our two mates: that Mr. Riach was sullen, unkind and harsh when he was sober, and Mr. Shuan would not hurt a fly except when he was drinking. I asked about the captain; but I was told drink made no difference to him.

One night, about eleven o'clock, Captain Hoseason came
down the ladder and addressed me.

"My man," said he, "we want ye to serve in the round-
house. You and Ransome are to change berths."

Even as he spoke, two seamen appeared in the scuttle,
carrying Ransome's body in their arms.

I brushed by the sailors and ran up the ladder on deck,
sickened by what I had seen of the poor boy. Quite clearly

Ransome was dead, murdered at the hand of Mr. Shuan in one of his fits of drunken cruelty.

The round-house, for which I was bound, and where I was now to sleep and serve, stood some six feet above the decks, and considering the size of the brig, was of good dimensions. Inside were a fixed table and bench, and two berths, one for the captain and the other for the two mates, turn and turn about. It was all fitted with lockers from top to bottom, so as to stow away the officers' belongings and part of the ship's stores; there was a second store-room underneath, which you entered by a hatchway in the middle of the deck; indeed, all the best of the meat and drink and the whole of the powder were collected in this place; and all the fire-arms, except the two pieces of brass ordnance, were set in a rack in the aftermost wall of the round-house. The most of the cutlasses were in another place. A small window with a shutter on each side, and skylight in the roof, gave it light by day; and after dark there was a lamp always burning.

My situation was anything but encouraging: there, in the round-house, I was doing dirty work for three men that I looked down upon, and one of whom, at least, should have hung upon a gallows; that was for the present; and as for the future, I could only see myself slaving alongside negroes in the tobacco fields.

More than a week went by, in which the ill-luck that had hitherto pursued the *Covenant* upon this voyage grew yet more strongly marked. About ten at night on the tenth day, when the brig was running south in a thick sea-mist, after rounding Cape Wrath, the ship struck and sank a small boat, from which only one person was saved.

Smallish in stature, but well set and as nimble as a goat, the newcomer wore costly clothes, and was armed with a pair of fine silver-mounted pistols and a great sword. He had a money-belt about his waist and explained to the captain that, as a loyal supporter of the Stewarts, he was taking it to help the Jacobite exiles in France, where he was in service with King Louis.

After some haggling, it was agreed that, in return for sixty guineas, the captain would set the stranger ashore; after which he would have to run the gauntlet of King George's troops, who were assisting the hated "Red Fox"—Colin Campbell of Glenure—to stamp out all the loyalty to the Stewart cause which still remained strong in the Western Highlands of Scotland.

When Hoseason and Riach had left me alone in the roundhouse, to serve our unexpected passenger with a meal, I discovered that I had need of the store-room key, and accordingly went in search of the captain. I found him talking to Riach, and heard enough of their conversation, before they became aware of my approach, to realize that the two of them were planning a treacherous attempt to rob the stranger.

"Captain," said I, "the gentleman is seeking a dram, and the bottle's out. Will you give me the key?"

"Why, here's our chance to get the fire-arms in the round-house!" Riach cried.

"Ay, ay!" put in Hoseason. "David, my man, see if you can fetch us a pistol or two and some powder, without arousing yon wild Hielandman's suspicions, and I give you my word that you shall have your fingers in that beltful of gold."

I told him that I would do as he wished and returned to the

round-house with the key. Walking up to the threatened Jacobite, as he sat eating at the table, I put my hand on his shoulder.

"Do ye want to be killed?" said I, and then told him all that I had heard.

"Will ye stand with me?" he asked.

"That will I!" said I.

"Why, then," said he, "what's your name?"

I told my new friend briefly about myself and he answered in kind, saying that his name was Stewart and that he was called Alan Breck. We then made hasty preparations to defend ourselves, in the round-house, from the attack which we knew must surely come.

And come it did, all of a sudden, with a rush of feet and a roar, and then a shout from Alan, and a sound of blows and some one crying out as if hurt. I looked back over my shoulder, and saw Mr. Shuan in the doorway crossing blades with Alan.

"That's him that killed the boy!" I cried.

"Look to your window!" said Alan; and as I turned back to my place, I saw him pass his sword through the mate's body.

It was none too soon for me to look to my own part; for my head was scarce back at the window, before five men, carrying a spare yard for a battering-ram, ran past me and took post to drive the door in. I had never fired with a pistol in my life, but it was now or never; and just as they swang the yard, I cried out, "Take that!" and shot into their midst.

I must have hit one of them, for he sang out, and then the whole party ran for it.

There was a short pause after that, but soon the captain and his murderous crew made a second assault on the round-house.

A knot of them made one rush of it, cutlass in hand, against the door; at the same moment, the glass of the skylight was dashed in a thousand pieces, and a man leaped through and landed on the floor. Before he got his feet, I had clapped a pistol to his back and shot him in the midst of the body.

I heard Alan shout as if for help, and saw that the door was thronged with faces. I thought we were lost, and catching up my cutlass, fell on them in flank. Alan, leaping back to get his distance, ran upon the sailors like a bull, roaring as he went. They broke before him like water, whilst the sword in his hands

flashed like quicksilver into the huddle of our fleeing enemies.

The round-house was like a shambles; three were dead inside, another lay in his death agony across the threshold; and there were Alan and I victorious and unhurt.

We were masters of the ship, and it was not long before the captain came to parley with Alan, who agreed to a truce provided that Hoseason obeyed his orders and set us down where we would be among friends.

Much against his better judgement, for he feared for his brig in the treacherous coastal waters, the captain set course for Loche Linnhe, and by nightfall the *Covenant* was rounding the south-west corner of the Island of Mull.

There, we fell foul of the Torran Rocks. For some time, clever seamanship on the part of Hoseason and Riach saved us from disaster; then, suddenly, the tide caught the brig and threw the wind out of her sails. She came round into the wind like a top, and struck the reef so hard that I was cast clean over the bulwarks into the sea.

I went down, and drank my fill, and then came up, and presently found I was holding to a spar, as the wild waters hurled me along. At last I reached the shore of an island and crawled ashore, wet, cold and weary. In the morning, I climbed a

hill to view my surroundings, but there was no sign of the brig and no evidence of life on the island, which proved to be a barren isle, called Earraid, lying off the coast of Mull and joined to it at low tide.

Hungry and miserable, I eventually found my way across to Mull, where I happened upon a kindly old gentleman who welcomed me to his roughly-built home, and gave me food, drink and a long night's rest, besides a message from Alan—who had safely escaped the wreck and passed by ahead of me—to follow him to Balachulish and from thence to the house of James of the Glens, at Aucharn in Duror of Appin.

Much refreshed, I set out on my journey and, a few days later, found myself being put ashore under the wood of Lettermore in Alan's county of Appin, south of Balachulish.

This was a wood of birches, growing on a steep, craggy side of a mountain that overhung the loch. A bridle-track ran north

and south through the midst of it, by the edge of which, where was a spring, I sat down to eat some oatbread and think upon my situation. What ought I to do, and why was I going to join myself with an outlaw like Alan?

As I was so sitting and thinking, a sound of men and horses came to me through the wood; and presently, at a turning of the road, I saw four travellers come into view. The first was a great, red-headed gentleman, of an imperious and flushed face; the second I correctly took to be a lawyer; the third was a servant; and the fourth a sheriff's officer.

I rose up from the bracken and asked the leading horseman if he could direct me to Aucharn.

"And what seek ye in Aucharn?" asked Colin Roy Campbell of Glenure; him they called the 'Red Fox'; for he it was, the hated henchman of King George, that I had stopped.

"The man that lives there," said I.

"James of the Glens," says Glenure musingly; and then to the lawyer: "Is he gathering his people, think ye?"

"Anyway," says the lawyer, "we shall do better to bide where we are, and let the soldiers rally us."

But, even as he spoke, there came the shot of a firelock from higher up the hill; and with the very sound of it Glenure fell upon the road.

"O, I am dead!" he cried, several times over.

I began to scramble up the hill, crying out, "The murderer! The murderer!" So little a time had elapsed, that when I got to the top of the first steepness, and could see some part of the open mountain, the murderer was still moving away at no great distance.

Below me, the lawyer and the sheriff's officer were standing just above the road, crying and waving on me to come back; and on their left, the redcoats, musket in hand, were beginning to struggle singly out of the lower wood.

"Why should I come back?" I cried. "Come you on!"

"Ten pounds if ye take that lad!" cried the lawyer. "He's an accomplice. He was posted here to hold us in talk."

The soldiers began to spread, some of them to run, and others to put up their pieces and cover me; and still I stood, so terrified by the turn of events that I felt unable to move.

"Duck in here among the trees," said a voice, close by. Indeed, I scarce knew what I was doing, but I obeyed; and as I did so, I heard the firelocks bang and the balls whistle in the birches.

Just inside the shelter of the trees I found Alan Breck standing, with a fishing-rod. "Come!" says he, and set off running along the side of the mountain towards Balachulish; and I, like a sheep, to follow him. Quarter of an hour later, Alan stopped, clapped down flat in the heather, and turned to me.

"Now," said he, "it's earnest. Do as I do, for your life."

And at the same speed, but now with infinitely more

precaution, we traced back across the mountain side by the same way that we had come, only perhaps higher; till at last Alan threw himself down in the upper wood of Lettermore, where I had found him at the first, and lay, with his face in the bracken, panting like a dog.

My own sides so ached, my head so swam, my tongue so hung out of my mouth with heat and dryness, that I lay beside him like one dead.

Alan was the first to come round. He rose, went to the border of the wood, peered out a little, and then returned and sat down.

"Well," said he, with a smile, "yon was a hot burst, David." Then Alan grew very grave, and said we had not much time to

throw away, but must both flee that country; he, because he was a deserter and a Jacobite, and the whole of Appin would now be searched like a chamber, and every one obliged to give a good account of himself; and I, because I was present at the murder, and was thought to be an accomplice.

"We're in the Hielands, David," he continued, "and ye'll receive nae justice if ye have to face fifteen Campbells in the jury-box. Nae doubt it's a hard thing to skulk and starve in the heather, but it's harder yet to lie shackled in a redcoat prison."

I asked Alan whither we should flee.

"We'll strike for Aucharn," he replied, "the house of my kinsman, James of the Glens, where I must get my clothes, and my arms, and money to carry us along; and then, David, we'll run for the Lowlands."

As we made across the wild countryside to Aucharn, each of us narrated his recent adventures. Alan told me that, after the brig had finally gone to the bottom, Hoseason ordered those of his seamen who had been saved to lay hands on him; Riach, however, took Alan's part, and so it was that he left the quarrelling crew of the *Covenant* to their own devices and found his way to Aucharn.

Night had fallen by the time we reached Aucharn and looked down upon the farmhouse from the top of a brae.

It seemed a house door stood open, letting out a beam of light; and all round the buildings people were moving hurriedly about, each carrying a lighted brand.

Alan whistled three times, in a particular manner, as we approached, and we were met at the yard gate by James Stewart himself. After greeting us, James of the Glens explained that all the activity was due to the murder of Colin Campbell.

"It will bring trouble on the country," he cried, wringing his hand, "and I am a man that has a family."

The faces of his servants in the torchlight were like those of

people overborne with hurry and panic, as they brought out hidden weapons of war and carried them away to be buried down the brae.

Finishing our business at the farmhouse quickly, Alan and I soon left the terrified folk at Aucharn, for, as Alan said to me: "The day comes unco soon in this month of July; and tomorrow there'll be a fine to-do with the redcoats, and it behoves you and me to be gone."

Sometimes we walked, sometimes ran; but, for all our hurry, dawn found us far from any shelter, in a rock-strewn valley down which ran a foaming river.

"This is no fit place for you and me," Alan said. "This is a place they're bound to watch."

And with that he ran harder than ever down to the waterside, in a part where the racing river was split in two among three rocks. Alan jumped clean upon the middle rock, and fell there on his hands and knees to check himself, for that rock was small and he might have pitched over on the far side. I had scarce time to measure the distance or to understand the peril before I had followed him, and he had caught and stopped me.

So there we stood, side by side, upon a small rock slippery with spray, a far broader leap in front of us, and the river dinning

upon all sides. When I saw where I was, there came on me a deadly sickness of fear, and I put my hand over my eyes.

"Hang or drown!" shouted Alan; and, turning his back upon me, he leaped over the farther branch of the stream, and landed safe.

I bent low on my knees and flung myself forth, with that kind of anger of despair that has sometimes stood me instead of courage. Sure enough, it was but my hands that reached the full length; I was sliddering back into the lynn, when Alan seized me, first by the hair, then by the collar, and with a great strain dragged me into safety.

Never a word he said, but set off running again for his life, and I must stagger to my feet and run after him. I had been weary before, but now I was sick and bruised.

At last Alan paused under a great rock that stood there among a number of others. By rights it was two rocks leaning together at the top, both some twenty feet high. Standing on my shoulders, Alan leaped up with such force as I thought must have

broken my collar-bone, and secured a lodgement. Once there, he let down his leathern girdle; and with the aid of that and a pair of shallow footholds in the rock, I scrambled up beside him.

Then I saw why we had come there; for the two rocks, being both somewhat hollow on the top and sloping one to the other, made a kind of dish or saucer, where as many as three or four men might have lain hidden.

There we two fugitives lay all day, with the sun beating upon us cruelly, and hardly daring to move or whisper, for fear of giving ourselves away to a force of redcoats who set up camp in the valley and posted sentries all around us.

At last, when the heat grew beyond bearing — and the soldiers had completed their search on our side of the valley — Alan and I dropped to the ground and began to slip from rock to rock, now crawling flat on our bellies, now making a run for it, heart in mouth.

By sundown, we had made some distance; and as soon as the shadow of night had fallen, we were able to stand our full height

and step out at a good pace of walking.

Our second brush with King George's soldiers took place when, striking east to win our way out of Appin, the region in which we were being sought, Alan and I entered a great stretch of moorland, surrounded by the tops of mountains from which our progress could be overlooked.

Sometimes, for half an hour together, we had to crawl from one heather bush to another, and the rest of the time it was necessary to walk stooping nearly to the knees.

About noon we lay down in a thick bush of heather to sleep. Alan took the first watch; and it seemed to me I had scarce closed

my eyes before I was shaken up to take the second. We had no
clock to go by; and Alan stuck a sprig in the ground to serve
instead; so that, as soon as the shadow of the bush should fall so
far to the east, I might know to rouse him. But I was by this time
so weary that I could have slept twelve hours at a stretch, and
every now and again I would give a jump and find I had been
dozing.

The last time I awoke, I could have cried aloud: for the sprig
made it clear that I had betrayed my trust. Then I looked out
around me on the moor, and my heart was like dying in my body,
for a troop of horse-soldiers had come down during my sleep, and

were drawing near to us from the south-east, spread out in the shape of a fan and riding their horses to and fro in the deep parts of the heather.

I waked Alan hastily and asked him what we ought to do.

"We'll have to play at being hares," said he, "and strike for Ben Alder, that wild, desert mountain to the north-east."

"But, Alan," cried I, "that will take us across the very coming of the soldiers!"

"I ken that fine," said he; "but if ye are driven back on Appin, we are two dead men."

With that he began to run forward on his hands and knees with an incredible quickness, as though it were his natural way of going. All the time, too, he kept winding in and out in the lower parts of the moorland where we were best concealed. Some of these had been burned or at least scathed with fire; and there rose in our faces a blinding, choking dust as fine as smoke. The aching and faintness of my body, the labouring of my heart, the soreness of my hands, and the smarting of my throat and eyes in the continual smoke of dust and ashes, had soon grown to be almost unbearable.

At length, in the first gloaming of the night, we heard a trumpet sound, and looking back from among the heather, saw the troop beginning to collect. A little after, they had built a fire and camped for the night, about the middle of the waste.

At this I begged and besought that we might lie down and sleep.

"There shall be no sleep the night!" said Alan. "From now on, these weary dragoons of yours will keep the crown of the muirland, and none will get out of Appin but winged fowls. We got through in the nick of time, and shall we endanger what we've gained? Na, na, when the day comes, it shall find you and me in a fast place on Ben Alder."

I became exhausted and ill as we staggered on through the night, and even Alan was in bad shape; but fortune smiled upon us, for we fell in with some out-sentries of Cluny Macpherson, a rebel chief whose clan guarded and supported him in his mountain hide-outs. To one of these refuges, called Cluny's Cage, we were led, and there received food, sleep and shelter until I was well enough to press on once more.

After many days of wearisome travelling over rough country, we finally reached the north bank of the Forth. Now there remained only one last barrier, the river itself, between us and safety. Once across, I could make myself known to my uncle's lawyer, Mr. Rankeillor, at Queensferry, tell him all that had happened and claim my inheritance.

The bridge at Stirling was guarded, so Alan and I tramped on eastwards until we reached a small place called Limekilns, opposite the town of Queensferry. There, at the little inn, we bought some bread and cheese from the daughter of the house.

She was so sorry for us, when we explained that I must visit Mr. Rankeillor but had no means of crossing the river, she agreed to row us across that night, as soon as her father was asleep.

This the kind lass duly did; and at dawn next day, I could be seen entering the long street of Queensferry, whilst Alan hid in the open country outside the town.

At this point, I realized suddenly that the task before me might well prove to be more difficult than I had previously supposed. I had to prove to Mr. Rankeillor that I was really David Balfour, and to do so in my ragged, dirty state would be no easy matter.

My luck, however, remained good; for, as I stopped before a fine-fronted house — uncertain as to how I should proceed — the door opened and there issued forth a shrewd, ruddy, kindly man in a well-powdered wig and spectacles. This gentleman was so much struck with my poor appearance that he came straight up to me and asked me what I did. I told him I was come on business, and asked him to direct me to the house of Mr. Rankeillor.

"Why," said he, "that is his house that I have just come out of; and I am that very man."

"Then, sir," said I, "I have to beg the favour of an interview."

"I do not know your name," said he, "nor yet your face."

"My name is David Balfour," said I.

"David Balfour?" he repeated, in rather a high tone, like one surprised. "And where have you come from, Mr. David Balfour?" he asked.

"I have come from a great many strange places, sir," said I; "but I think it would be as well to tell you where and how in a more private manner."

"Yes," says he, "that will be the best, no doubt." And he led me back with him into his house, cried out to someone whom I could not see that he would be engaged all morning, and brought me into a little dusty chamber full of books and

documents. "And now," says he, "if you have any business, pray be brief and come swiftly to the point."

Whereupon, I told the good lawyer all that I knew of myself, my uncle and Shaws, of the claim I had upon that estate, and indeed of my adventures since the day on which I was kidnapped aboard the *Covenant* by order of my wicked relation.

To this Mr. Rankeillor listened with great attention; and at the end of it all, the two of us came to trust each other. The lawyer then explained that, whilst I had been fleeing for my life from the Highlands, much concerning me had been brought to his notice.

My old friend Mr. Campbell, the minister of Essendean, having heard nothing from me, had called upon Mr. Rankeillor, and together they had visited Uncle Ebenezer. He spun them a yarn as to my whereabouts, but was soon found to be lying, when Captain Hoseason reached Queensferry with the story of my drowning in the wreck of the *Covenant*.

At last, when we had reached a thoroughly friendly understanding, Mr. Rankeillor rose, called over the stair to lay another

plate, for Mr. Balfour would stay to dinner, and led me into a bedroom in the upper part of the house. Here he set before me water and soap, and a comb; and laid out some clothes that belonged to his son; and here he left me to my toilet.

When I had done, Mr. Rankeillor told me how it was that my father, through love of my mother, had moved away from Shaws and left the estate in the hands of his brother, Ebenezer; my uncle had then become a selfish old miser, and ill-used both the property and the tenants whose living depended upon it.

"Well, sir," said I, "and in all this, what is my position?"

"The estate is yours beyond a doubt," replied the lawyer. "But a lawsuit would be expensive, and your recent doings in the Highlands might come to light during the course of legal action. My advice, therefore, is to make a very easy bargain with your uncle, perhaps even leaving him at Shaws, and contenting your-self in the meanwhile with a fair provision."

I told him I was very willing to be easy. "The great affair," I asked, "is to bring home to my uncle the kidnapping?"

"Surely," said Mr. Rankeillor.

"Well, sir," said I, "here is my way of it." And I opened my plot to him.

When everything had been agreed, he got a sheet of paper and a pencil, and set to work writing and weighing every word; and at last touched a bell and had his clerk into the chamber.

"Torrance," said he, "I must have this written out fair against tonight; and when it is done, you will be so kind as put on your hat and be ready to come along with this gentleman and me, for you will probably be wanted as a witness."

That evening the three of us met Alan, at the place agreed upon, and explained the plot to him.

He was to call upon Uncle Ebenezer at Shaws and, pretending to have been in league with Captain Hoseason over the matter of my kidnapping, trap the old miser into admitting that he had planned and paid to have me carried away as a slave aboard the *Covenant*.

Alan, good friend that he was, accepted the part we asked him to play, and presented himself that very night at the door of Shaws, whilst Mr. Rankeillor, Torrance and I crouched down beside the corner of the house to be witnesses to what followed.

My uncle answered Alan's heavy knocking upon the door, and was soon entangled in the web which his visitor's clever tongue spun for him. At last Alan wrung from Uncle Ebenezer the words

that we were waiting to hear.

"I'll be perfectly honest with ye," said he, "Hoseason was to have the selling of David in Carolina."

"That will do excellently well," said Mr. Rankeillor, stepping forward with Torrance and myself. Never a word said my uncle, for he knew now that he had betrayed himself and would have to accept our terms.

We all entered the house, and there the lawyer had little trouble in securing Uncle Ebenezer's signature to the document that had been drawn up earlier in the day. By the terms of this, he bound himself to satisfy Rankeillor as to his business dealings, and to pay me two clear thirds of the yearly income of Shaws.

So, at last, I came into my inheritance, and it was now my clear duty to help Alan to leave the country and return to France.

Next day, Mr. Rankeillor gave me a letter to his bankers, the British Linen Company in Edinburgh, placing a credit to my name. Armed with this I set out with Alan for the city. There, the bank would supply me with money, and I could then seek out a lawyer who was an Appin Stewart, and a man therefore to be wholly trusted; and it should be his part to find a ship and to arrange for Alan's safe embarkation.

When we drew near to Edinburgh, it was arranged that Alan should live here and there in the country, visiting a particular place each day for news of the plans being laid for his escape.

And now we stopped, in view of the city, with its great castle on the hill, for both of us knew that we had come to where our ways parted.

"Well, goodbye," said Alan, holding out his hand.

"Goodbye," said I, and gave the hand a little grasp.

A moment later, saddened more than I can say by the parting, I had started down hill towards the city, to seek the British Linen Company's bank.